FIFTY ON FIFTY

FIFTY REASONS WHY
WE LOVE MR. FIFTY

A. Kim Weston

abbott press®

A DIVISION OF WRITER'S DIGEST

Fifty on Fifty
Fifty Reasons Why We Love Mr. Fifty

ISBN: 978-1-4582-0531-5 (sc)
ISBN: 978-1-4582-0532-2 (e)

Library of Congress Control Number: 2012913412

Abbott Press books may be ordered through booksellers or by contacting:

Abbott Press
1663 Liberty Drive
Bloomington, IN 47403
www.abbottpress.com
Phone: 1-866-697-5310

Printed in the United States of America

Abbott Press rev. date: 7/31/2012

1. He Looks Like a Greek God

Who wouldn't want a Greek god? Broad shoulders, tan skin, six-pack abs, slim hips, that perfect V just above the waist of his jeans and a small amount of chest hair to run your fingers through. Not the hairy Italian or German sausage we all have at home who looks like a human sweater, but 100 percent lean Greek god beef!

2.   He Has More Money Than God

Yes, yes, we want money and we want lots of it and we aren't ashamed to admit it! We would love to wear $600 panties that our men rip off with one flick of the wrist, just so we can go out and buy even more panties for them to rip off.

3. He Knows How to Twiddle His Thumbs

We now look at a man's thumbs with an entirely new appreciation for what those two digits can do. With thumbs added to the equation, size truly doesn't matter. Christian Grey's thumbs bring new meaning to the phrase, "Two thumbs up!" Maybe now we should start saying, "Two thumbs in!"

4. He Has Wine Every Night with Dinner

We love wine. We enjoy wine and would really enjoy having a man ask us every night what kind of wine we would like with dinner, not just if we would like wine with dinner. Hell, we would enjoy drinking wine with lunch every day too the way Christian enjoys it. Oh, and those afternoon treats to celebrate our fifth orgasm of the day. "Way to come for me Baby. Would you like a glass of Pinot to celebrate?"

5.   He Likes a Girl Who Eats

Finally, a man who wants a girl to finish her entire plate of food! Not only her entire meal, but eat dessert too! Oh, and then another dessert later. We all wish we had Christian Grey flavored popsicles at home, big on flavor, low in calories!

6. He Can Fill Up a Pair of Boxers

Refer to Number 3 ladies. Who said size doesn't mean anything? That it's quality over quantity? That it's more important what he can do with it rather than if he can tickle your cervix with it? Yes, yes, that last one is true, but we're sorry, no one wants a Vienna sausage in bed. If we want something that small, we will keep with the thumbs.

7.   He Knows How to Dress

We love a man in a suit. How refreshing would it be to see our men dressed as gentlemen rather than in whatever they picked up from the floor? Or, better yet, to actually notice that our men own something other than T-shirts, shorts and sneakers? Even an Italian or German sausage would look more appetizing dressed in the right packaging.

8.   He Knows How to Wear a Necktie

And we're not talking about around his neck. How about the way he ties it around our wrists or our ankles, or even possibly around his penis? Oh, around that large Greek god penis! Yes, a long tie would be in order under those circumstances, and it wouldn't even have to be gray.

9.   He Likes Bubble Baths

Not only does he like bubble baths with his woman, he likes to *drink wine* while he's taking a bubble bath with his woman! And what about the way he can use a washcloth? There is something extremely sexy about getting washed by a Greek god in a bubble bath. Or wait: *washing* a Greek god in a bubble bath is even sexier! Let's hope we have a large enough washcloth for *down there*.

10.   He Knows How to Buy Jewelry

Not the 70 percent off Kmart special, but the real deal from Cartier, for no reason whatsoever other than because he wants to. Unless of course it's a prize he gives us for the great blow job we gave him the night before, or two hours before, or right there in the damn parking lot of the jewelry store!

11. He Understands the Meaning of Retail Therapy

We can shop for as long as we want and wherever we want and he won't allow us to pay for anything. We don't even have to find a good sale; we can pay full price! "What a great blow job honey. Now go buy yourself something, and don't forget to take my credit card!"

12. He Likes Brunettes Because They're More Fun

Finally, brunettes rule! Being blonde is way overrated anyway. We brunettes are known to have a few tricks up our sleeves, and we've even been known to have minimal gag reflexes, which deserves even more expensive jewelry!

13.   He Can Dance

And dance, and dance, and dance, and he actually enjoys it. We don't mean that wild bouncing, up-and-down dancing, but *dancing:* glide-us-around-the-floor-like-he's-making-love-to-us dancing. Talk about the ultimate foreplay to get us worked up. All the bouncing, up-and-down, *grinding* kind of dancing is saved for later while in bed, or in the tub, or on the marble foyer floor, or in the car, or in the kitchen, or on the piano, or...

14. He Will Spend $100,000 for a Single Dance

At that price, he can even step on our feet, drop us, or fuck us right there on the dance floor! "Excuse me, Miss? Would you care to fuck? I mean, dance?"

15.   He Loves All Types of Music

And he loves to do all sorts of fun things while he listens to music! "What music would you like to come to tonight, my dear?"

16.   He Practices Safe Sex

He practices *a lot* of safe sex! They better not run out of extra large packets of foil where he shops. Oh my. Who thought that the sound of ripping foil could be so sexy? It makes us want to play with some Reynolds Wrap.

17. He Loves to Make Love to Your Feet

If you have a foot fetish, he's your man! Hell, even if you don't have a foot fetish, he's your man. You would soon get a foot fetish after what he can do to your feet! "And this little piggy said, 'Oh my fucking God,' all the way home!"

18. He Likes a Girl to Wear Fuck Me Shoes

Expensive fuck me shoes that he pays for! It's good to wear fuck me high heels that torture our feet because then all the little piggies are ready to have their very own orgasms, administered of course by those miraculous Greek god thumbs.

19. He Is Very Protective of Those He Loves

Buying us the safest car on the market is so endearing. Buying us the safest car on the market with all the amenities is even more endearing. Fucking us in that expensive car is priceless.

20. He Holds His Lover Close in Public

How sweet is it to be held close to our Greek god while in public so that everyone knows we belong to him and that he adores us. Making all of the other women jealous, however, is even sweeter! "Yes, he is mine, and yes, I did come three times this morning before breakfast. Eat your heart out, bitch!"

21. He Understands the Magnetism of Elevators

Oh what can be done in such close quarters while riding down seventy-six floors. We look at elevators now in a whole new light. We look at what's coming out of elevators even more closely, just in case a mega-rich Greek god wearing a suit and gray tie walks out of it!

22. He Knows How to Give a Girl Flowers

Who said that a room full of flowers isn't romantic? Who said that fucking on a petal-covered floor of a boathouse isn't romantic? Who said that fucking in a meadow full of wildflowers isn't romantic? Who the fuck cares? The only petal we're interested in is the one between Christian's legs!

23. He Has JFH

Just-fucked hair never sounded so sexy. It looks even better on a Greek god wearing a suit, especially if we are the reason for his hair looking just-fucked!

"Dude, what's up with your hair?"

"Oh, that. I just had the best fuck of my life with the most beautiful goddess in the universe."

24. He Can Fly a Helicopter and a Glider

We all want to chase the dawn in a glider and then chase the dusk in a helicopter! The only problem is that Christian's so busy being the pilot, he can't help us chase an orgasm while we're up there!

25.   He Uses the Right Type of Balls for Playtime

While our German or Italian sausages are out playing with soccer balls, or footballs, or basketballs, or golf balls, the Greek god we all lust over is keeping us happy indoors with our balls of choice: warm, wet and silver! Now we truly understand the importance of kegals!

26. He Can Make "Laters Baby" Sound So Sexy

And cute, and romantic, and fun, and endearing, and exciting, and suspenseful! It makes us wonder just how many orgasms we will have *laters*.

27.   He Can Play the Piano

Playing us *on* the piano is more enticing! Who out there has always wanted to bang the piano keys with their feet while getting banged by a Greek god? Talk about making beautiful music together!

28. He Can Play a Fun Game of Pool

Refer to Number 27 ladies, but instead think about the pool table and Christian's big stick. It's all too obvious into which pocket we would like him to sink his shot!

29. He Likes Kinky Fuckery

He likes it in the playroom, on the piano, on the pool table, in the catamaran, in the Audi, on the staircase, on the countertop. We too would love to deface every single surface of his condo with him, tied up or not.

30. He Has Extraordinary Fine Motor Skills and Dexterity of the Fingers

Oh what those finely honed fingers can do in an elevator! They run a close second to those thumbs!

31.   He Likes the Taste of Salty Fish

Think about what Christian does with those thumbs and fingers of his and you'll know what this one means. "Hey honey, what's for dinner?" "Fish!"

32. He Enjoys Giving Out As for a Job Well Done

We hope we never graduate. Can we add more classes to our curricu-come? Oh, sorry, curriculum? It's official; we are all striving to make the honor roll.

33. He Likes When We Come First

He doesn't mind if we come last, either. We can come in between, too, if we'd like.

34. He Skips Third Base and Goes Straight for Home

Batter up! Baseball never sounded better. It gives us a new appreciation of the term, "Play ball!" Now we understand why it's America's favorite pastime. Of course, it doesn't hurt that Christian plays with such a big bat.

35. He Knows the True Meaning of a Picnic

To hell with the food and the wine, the gorgeous weather and the beautiful scenery. Christian only wants *us* for the picnic, right there in the middle of a meadow. What's the perfect picnic food for our Greek god? Fish!

36. He Is a Fantastic Palm Reader

We now have a new appreciation for palms too. "I see another orgasm in your future." Still like those thumbs though.

37. He Dumps a Bitchy Female Friend Because We Want Him To

It's the ultimate proof of love. After that, he deserves for us to swallow: our ultimate proof of love. Looks like another trip to Cartier is in order!

38. He Loves Ice Cream

Ice cream sounds good right about now. Vanilla ice cream sounds *really* good right about now! Who cares about having to wash the sheets? Bring it on!

39. He Has Legitimate Reasons for Being on the Emotional Level of a Four-Year-Old

As opposed to the emotional "four-year-olds" we are married to, engaged to, or dating.

40. He Is Not Afraid of Therapy

He actually wants to act older than a four-year-old and not have us be his mother. How refreshing is that?

41.　He Wants to End World Hunger

Of course, he wants to do that while ending his own hunger for *us*. Luckily, Christian has quite the appetite!

42. He Looks Good in Torn Blue Jeans

But then again, Greek gods look good in anything. Naturally, it helps knowing *where* he wears the tears into his jeans. "Damn, you look so hot chained to my four-poster bed, my hard-on tore a hole in my jeans!"

43. He Makes "Come for Me, Baby" the Sexiest Statement on the Planet

Goes to show how hard Christian works at keeping us happy. Words we would never get tired of hearing! And if we aren't happy, we can always go shopping, or drink wine, or eat ice cream!

44. He Loves His Parents and Siblings

This makes Christian incredibly sexy and even more endearing in our eyes. So sexy and endearing, in fact, that he would once again earn our ultimate proof of love from Number 37.

45.   He Can Read Our Minds and Finish Our Thoughts

"Christian, how did you know I want to come again? Wow, it's so amazing that you knew exactly what I was thinking!"

46. He Takes His Work Seriously

Thankfully, he considers his main job to be making us orgasm a jillion times in one night, *after* we drink wine, eat a full meal, and have ice cream in bed.

47. He Always Gets What He Wants

Us naked and continually coming is what he always wants: anytime, anywhere, anyplace, especially in elevators.

48. He Has a Full Staff to Fulfill All Our Needs

Not just *that* staff, but a housekeeper, a cook, a driver, a personal shopper, and a security team to boot!

49. He Doesn't Want Us to Work

We can work all we want on having incredible orgasms, but we don't have to *work*. Time to update our resume for the most awesome job on the planet: sex goddess to Christian Grey!

50. He Doesn't Believe in Signing a Prenup

Need we say more?